CW00867458

THE MAKING OF A MAGE

A WOLVES OF VIMAR PREQUEL

V. M. SANG

Copyright (C) 2021 V.M. Sang

Layout design and Copyright (C) 2021 by Next Chapter

Published 2021 by Shadow City – A Next Chapter Imprint

Edited by Elizabeth N. Love

Cover art by Cover Mint

To all of the authors at Next Chapter. You are an amazing group of people who give such great support to each other.

CHAPTER ONE

CARTHINAL, ACCOMPANIED BY HIS NANNY, BLENDIN, dragged his feet as he entered the house.

They were on their way home from his grandfather's funeral. The old man had passed away from a heart attack the previous week, yet he had seemed full of life up until then. Carthinal could not understand what had happened. His grandfather was the only relative he had in Bluehaven, his parents and his grandmother having died. Now he was all alone in the world.

His father had been an elf, and although sixteen and nominally of age, Carthinal's progress was slower than true humans. He appeared—in both physical and mental development—to be a young boy of eleven.

He wandered around the house, his steps echoing in empty rooms. His grandfather's study looked, to the young boy, to be darker than usual, in spite of the sun streaming in through the windows. Silence filled rooms where he had enjoyed conversations with his grandparents. All life had gone from the house with the death of his grandfather. Now it was just a building where it had once been a home.

Carthinal went into the garden. He sat on his swing and swung idly backward and forward. What would happen to him now? Would they send him to his father's people in Rindisillaron? It was a long way away, and he had no recollection of his paternal grandparents, although they had been in Bluehaven when he had been born.

He looked at the house. He heard the laughter of his grandmother and his grandfather's deep voice. He even thought he heard his mother calling to him, although both his parents had been dead for the past eight years. He jumped off the swing and picked up a stick.

Clenching his jaw so tightly that it hurt, he slashed at the plants as he spat words out through his gritted teeth. "Why did they all die and leave me?" But ruining the garden gave him little satisfaction.

Blendin came out and found him still destroying the plants. "Come, Master Carthinal. This won't help. You need to come in and have something to eat."

"Shan't! I'm not hungry." He slashed at a tulip.

"What have those poor flowers done to you? You know you'll be sorry once you've calmed down."

"I don't want to go back into the house." He stamped his foot. "There's no one there. It's dead. Just like Mother and Father, Grandmother and Grandfather."

Blendin sat down on a bench and pulled the boy towards her, holding him tight.

He kicked out at her and tried to bite, but she held him close. "This is now your house, Carthinal." She ignored his struggles. "Your grandfather left it to you in his will. You're a rich young man. If you no longer want to live here, you can sell it and buy somewhere else."

Looking into the boy's deep blue, almost indigo eyes,

Blendin saw the hurt he felt. She brushed his auburn hair from his face and led him back inside.

The servants worked as usual. Carthinal's grandfather had arranged that money should be sent to Promin, the butler, who then paid the other servants. Carthinal had his meals in the nursery with Blendin, although Promin had said that, as the master of the house, he should eat in the dining room. Carthinal could not bring himself to eat alone in that large room.

The days passed. Gromblo Grimnor, the lawyer who dealt with his grandfather's affairs, often appeared at the house.

Carthinal found him in his grandfather's study one day.

"What are you doing?" the boy asked, frowning. "Why are you here? You've been coming a lot recently."

Gromblo Grimnor smiled with his mouth, but it did not reach his eyes. He looked Carthinal up and down. "There are a lot of loose ends to tidy up, child. I need to come here to find things out."

"What sort of things?"

"Things you wouldn't understand, boy. Lawyer things."

Although sixteen, Carthinal had always been treated as a child, and so he turned and left the lawyer to do what he needed to do. The law did not know what to do about a boy whose chronological age said he was an adult, but whose development said he was a child.

Every day he walked around the town. Being in the house had become too painful. Sometimes he stayed out all day. There was no one at the house for him to talk to now. He considered going back to the school where his grandfather had sent him, but they, like everyone else, did not want a sixteen-year-old who looked and behaved as if he were eleven. His grandfather's money and influence had kept him there, but now, they didn't want him.

Visits by Gromblo Grimnor increased. Carthinal asked Promin why the lawyer was there so often. The butler shrugged and shook his head.

Blendin had no idea either. "I don't know the workings of the law. Perhaps it's because your grandfather died so suddenly, or because he was well off. Or it might even be because of you. You are an adult in Grosmer law, but still a child, in reality. That's a bit confusing for the lawyers."

One day, when Carthinal had been out for hours, he returned to find the door locked against him. Gromblo Grimnor appeared when he knocked.

"Go away," the lawyer said. "There's nothing for you here. We don't want beggars at the door."

The boy crossed the road and stood looking at the house he had once called home. Some men came and erected a sign saying it was for sale. How could they sell his house without his permission? His grandfather left it to him in his will.

Carthinal sat on a wall. As he watched, the staff who had served his grandparents, left one by one. Some carried bags, others nothing. All turned to look back at the house as they trudged away. None saw the small auburn-haired lad sitting on the wall.

When he had seen everyone leave except the lawyer, Carthinal turned away. Where should he go? He had no living relatives. Not here in Bluehaven, anyway. He had relatives in the elven homeland of Rindisillaron, but he had no idea how to get there, nor how to find his paternal grandparents if he did manage it.

He ambled away, constantly turning to look toward the house. He had no idea where he was going, but staying there was pointless. His stomach rumbled. By now, the cook would have given him some honey cakes to assuage his hunger until it was time for the evening meal. His mouth felt dry, too.

He had a little money in his pocket and he wended his way toward the market place where there would be stalls selling food. He did not know what his small amount would buy him.

Sixteen was the legal age of majority in Grosmer, but Carthinal did not feel grown up. No one knew when he would be able to take on the responsibilities of an adult. Elves were twenty-five before they became officially adults, but a half-elf—well, no one knew. Many people found his slow development odd and thought he was mentally deficient, that a sixteen-year-old should look and behave as if he were only eleven.

Carthinal arrived at the market. Taking a few coins from his pocket, he wandered past the stalls looking for something he could afford.

He stopped by a stall. "How much are your small pies?"

"The very small ones are one royal," the stallholder replied, citing one of the copper coins.

"Please may I have one?"

The man smiled and passed a pie to the child. "Don't spoil your evening meal with it, though, or your parents will be annoyed with me."

Carthinal's indigo blue eyes filled with tears, and he turned away so the man would not see. He strolled to the park gates, munching on the pie. Where would he sleep tonight? Would it be safe to sleep outdoors? All these questions passed through his mind as he finished the pie and brushed the crumbs off his tunic.

As the grandson of a prominent guild member in the town of Bluehaven, Carthinal had always been well dressed. Today was no exception. He wore a dark green tunic over a lighter green shirt and brown trousers. The cut and the cloth marked him out as the child of a wealthy family. He had never known hardship in his entire life.

As he passed a fountain, he cupped his hands and picked up some of the water. After slaking his thirst, he entered the park gates. Fortunately, it was summer, and so the night would not be cold. Carthinal sat down on the grass. What would happen to him now? He had no home. How would he survive?

CHAPTER TWO

As darkness approached, Carthinal fell asleep where he sat on a grassy bank, shaded by a large tree. He dreamed of his grandfather. They were in his office and the old man spoke to the child standing in front of him.

"Carthinal, remember this. Life isn't always easy. You've been lucky. You've never known hardship. The gods be praised you never will, but everything will not go smoothly, even so." His grandfather sat on a chair in front of his desk and pulled Carthinal toward him, putting his arms around the child. "When you meet problems, always think them through. Take your time, and don't try to rush things. If you do that, it will usually turn out right in the end."

The sun woke Carthinal the next morning. He stretched, looked around and wondered where he was, and why he wasn't in his bed. Then he remembered. He had no home now. His eyes began to fill with tears, but he brushed them away.

His stomach rumbled as he stood and made his way back to the marketplace. He bought some fruit for one royal and a small glass of goats' milk for another.

The sun rose high in the sky and Carthinal returned to the park where he sat in the shade of a tall tree. This far south in the land of Grosmer, summers were hot, and soon the young lad began to feel thirsty. He stood and made his way back to the fountain where he drank some more water before wandering once more toward the market place.

At noon, he bought some bread filled with chicken. He looked at the coins remaining in his hand. Only three royals. He could only get a couple more meals with them. What would he do then? He could get water to drink, but that wouldn't help him beat off starvation.

He wandered the streets of Bluehaven all day until he found himself outside the offices belonging to the lawyer his grandfather had trusted with his will. He crossed the road and opened the door.

The young woman sitting at a desk looked up.

"What do you want?" she snapped. "This is a lawyer's office, not a child's playground. Be off with you."

Carthinal stood his ground. "I want to speak with Gromblo Grimnor, please."

The girl laughed. "And what business have you with a lawyer?"

"I want my home back." Carthinal sat on a bench situated against a wall.

"A child can't own a house."

"I'm sixteen."

The woman laughed. "Sixteen? You look no more than eleven. Be a good boy and go away. Find your friends and play."

"I'm not moving from here until I see the lawyer." Carthinal set his mouth in a straight line.

The woman stood and rounded her desk. She took Carthinal by the arm and tried to propel him to the door. He planted his feet onto the ground and pulled back. The woman slipped and almost fell. She cried out.

A door behind the woman's desk opened. "What's all the noise about, Hiroma?" The man who stood in the doorway caught sight of Carthinal. His face reddened and his hands formed fists at his side. His eyes slid from side to side.

"What do you want?" he growled.

Carthinal's mouth formed a firm line. "I want my house back."

"What are you talking about, boy? You are, what? Eleven years old? How can an eleven-year-old have a house? Go back to your parents."

"I have no parents. And I'm sixteen."

Gromblo Grimnor laughed. "Sixteen? Sixteen? I've seen taller thirteen-year-olds than you. Don't try to kid me. Now, what do you really want? And who sent you? Do you want money? If you're in some gang, they've not done very well with this scam."

"You know who I am." Carthinal looked Gromblo in the eye. "I am Carthinal. My grandfather was Kendo Borlin. He left his house and money to me. He told me so."

Gromblo narrowed his eyes. "So that's your game. Trying to impersonate Carthinal. Well, I have to tell you that Carthinal is dead. He died of pneumonia last year. Some say his death was the cause of his Grandfather's illness—that the old man never recovered from the shock. So, you see, you can't be Carthinal." The lawyer laughed.

"I'm not dead. I'm here. And I want to know why you stole my home."

Gromblo turned to Hiroma. "Go and call the guards. We need to get this child out of here."

As she left, Carthinal felt a tightness in his chest, and a familiar feeling welling up from his stomach. Clenching his fists, he ran at Gromblo and kicked him in the shins. The lawyer yelled, hopped on one leg for a few seconds and lunged at Carthinal, who slipped beneath his arm. Steadying himself on the wall behind the bench where Carthinal had been sitting, he turned and, with a roar, launched himself once more at the child. This time he managed to catch Carthinal's arm. Carthinal bit the hand holding him, but Gromblo managed to hang on to the boy.

Carthinal screamed at the man. "I'm not dead. I'm here, and you've stolen my home and my money."

The door opened and Hiroma appeared with a guard.

"What's going on here?" the guard asked.

"This little rat is trying to say he's Kendo Borlin's grandson. You know, the head of the guilds, who died earlier this year? I think he's trying to get money from me."

"Too right I am. You owe me a fortune."

Gromblo turned to the guard. "See what I mean? I grant you he looks a bit like Carthinal, with the red hair and blue eyes, but that child is dead."

"Do you have proof of the child's death?"

Carthinal looked at the guard. He had not thought of that. There could not be anything to prove the demise of Carthinal. He stood right here in front of them, very much alive.

Gromblo turned to Hiroma. "Go and get the Borlin file."

The young woman left, to return a few minutes later with a thick file. Gromblo took it and laid it on his secretary's desk.

He fumbled through the papers then pulled one out. "I did a lot of work for Kendo Borlin Aha! Here's the paper giving details of Carthinal's death. Very sad it was. A lovely little boy. Such a sweet nature."

Carthinal frowned. He had hardly ever seen Gromblo when he visited his grandfather. Neither had he ever heard himself described as having a "sweet nature." He had been too much of a rebel and short-tempered for that epithet to be applied.

The guard looked at the paper. He frowned. "Looks as if the name could have been scrubbed out."

Gromblo paled. "Well, you know how it is. Secretaries aren't like they used to be." He flashed a look at Hiroma who started tapping her foot. "I expect she made a spelling mistake or something."

The guard grunted. Carthinal thought he saw something pass between the guard and Gromblo as the guard handed the paper back, but he could not be sure. The guard grabbed him and propelled him towards the door, pushing him so that Carthinal rolled over in the dust in the road.

"Get out of here." The guard gave him another push, but more gently this time. "I don't want to see you anywhere near here in future. That lawyer's sneaky, not like the old man who used to be there. He'll try to do you harm if I'm not mistaken."

With that, the guard stomped away, looking at something in his hand.

Carthinal watched as the guard disappeared round the corner of a building. What did he mean? Did he mean he believed Carthinal and not Gromblo? He shook his head and put the thought away.

Carthinal made his way back to the park where he had slept and sat on the grass. He pulled out what money he had left. As he counted it, a shadow loomed over him. Carthinal looked up. A boy of about fifteen stood there, with another standing behind him.

"'And over yer money."

Carthinal jumped to his feet, stuffing the coins back into his pocket. "No! Why should I?"

The boy was much bigger than Carthinal. In fact, he stood a head taller, and he was broad-shouldered. His friend was a little smaller, but not by much.

"Because if yer don't, we'll punch yer until y' bleedin' well drop it, then we'll get it anyway. Your choice."

Carthinal backed away, keeping his eyes on both boys as best he could and his hand on the coins in his pocket. If he gave these thugs his money, he would have nothing to buy food with. He would starve.

They both came at him at once. Being smaller, Carthinal managed to duck under both their hands but felt a blow on the back of his head. He went down but kicked out his feet as he did so. The second boy, as luck would have it, happened to be coming in for another blow. Carthinal's kick took both his legs from under him. He crashed down on top of his victim.

The first boy dragged his friend off, but the blow Carthinal expected did not come. He looked up to see his assailant held in a firm grip by another, even larger boy, while a smaller one pummelled the second.

Carthinal's nostrils flared and he clenched his fists. How dare these young thugs try to steal his money? Taking advantage of the fact that the larger of his two assailants was held, he bunched his fist and slammed it into his midriff. The boy holding him swung him round and punched him as well. Gasping for breath, the boy took off, running as fast as his legs could carry him.

The smaller of the two new arrivals dipped and dodged and got in quite a lot of blow without being hit himself, but as soon as his opponent saw his friend running, he, too, turned on his heels and fled.

Panting, the smaller of his rescuers turned to Carthinal.

"Right. 'Oo are yer and what in the name of Zol's balls are yer doin' on our patch?"

Carthinal frowned. "Patch? I don't understand."

"Yer not part o' our gang, and yer not part o' th' bloody Green Fish, either. So 'oo are yer?"

"Green Fish?"

The boy frowned and ran his fingers through his dark hair. "Start by tellin' me 'oo you are. Bull, 'old 'im t'make sure 'e don't make a bleedin' run for it. Right. We've never seen yer 'ere afore. Tell me, 'oo are yer?"

"I'm Carthinal Borlin. I live, or rather used to live, up on the hill."

"A blasted rich kid," Bull growled. "Let's kick 'im."

"I'm not a rich kid. Not anymore." Carthinal looked at the ground.

The smaller boy put his head on one side. "What d'yer mean, 'anymore'?"

"The lawyer's taken my home and said I'm dead. He had a paper to prove it."

Bull released Carthinal's arms. "What d'yer think, Cat? Let 'im go?"

Cat shook his head. "'E's not part o' Green Fish. We can't 'ave 'im wanderin' round our bleedin' territory, operatin' on 'is own. We'll take 'im to 'eadquarters. Rooster'll decide what ter do wi' 'im. Anyroad, we can't leave 'im 'ere. 'E's just a kid. Green Fish'll make mincemeat of 'im.'E'll never bleedin' survive."

Carthinal did not know what they were talking about, but as he had no other ideas about what he could do, he followed the pair.

They led him to an area Carthinal had never been before, near the docks. It was rundown. He wrinkled his nose at the smell of rotting food lying in the gutters and carefully skirted other unidentifiable things. Carthinal did not want to know what they were. Bull and Cat paid no heed to the debris in the road and walked straight through whatever lay there.

A skinny dog barked at them as they passed, and half-starved cats jumped onto the walls. Dirty children ran wild in the streets, shouting and throwing things at the cats.

Carthinal hung back. He did not feel comfortable here. People looked suspiciously at his expensive, if dirty, clothes. One man, with a menacing look on his face, made to approach Carthinal as he trailed behind the other two.

Cat looked back. "Kassilla's tits, man, 'e's wi' us. Leave 'im alone."

The man stared at Cat. "Where're yer takin' 'im? 'E's a bleedin' toff. Rooster'll not thank yer fer bringin' a toff to yer 'eadquarters—showin' 'im where yer all 'ang out. I bet 'e'll go ter th' bleedin' guard as soon as 'e gets back ter his own folks."

"You mind yer own bloody business, Framnil. Rooster'll decide, not you."

Carthinal shivered. He did not like this place. People here mistrusted rich folk. He looked around. Eyes peered from windows, and everyone not indoors had stopped, watching with hostility. Cat and Bull were not much older than he was, although they did look their age. Carthinal estimated them to be around fifteen or sixteen. If the people turned ugly, how could these boys fight back? These people didn't know he had no money and was now as destitute as they were.

He looked at the narrow alleys. The houses crowded together so there was not much sun reaching these streets. Anyone or anything could be lurking in those shadows. He wrapped his arms around himself as he tried to make out anything hiding in the gloom.

Cat turned to Carthinal, ignoring the people. "Come on,

you. We need to see Rooster." He began walking away. Carthinal followed, but not without a glance back.

Bull noticed. "Dunna be afeared. Them'll not do nuffin'. They's afeard o' Rooster an' th' gang."

They came to a dark alley where his escorts turned off the main road. A short way along they arrived at a door whose paint had mostly peeled off. Cat knocked a complex pattern and the door opened a crack—just enough for Carthinal to see a grey eye peering out.

"Oh, it's you." The voice was female. Carthinal saw the eye turn to him. "'Oo's this?"

"Someone 'oo might want to join us."

Carthinal opened his mouth to say that he did not want to join a criminal gang, but Cat spoke again to the girl.

"Come on, Shrew. Open up. We need to see Rooster."

The door creaked on its hinges as Shrew swung it back. The three entered a long corridor.

Carthinal looked around. Inside it appeared cleaner than outside. The wooden planks on the floor had been polished and the walls looked clean and painted. Doors, clean and white, opened off the corridor, with a door at the end that stood open.

"Come on. Rooster'll want to see yer, but take yer boots off first." Shrew pointed to a shoe stand by the door. "Squirrel'll skin me alive if I let yer trail mud over 'er scrubbed floor."

When they had removed their footwear, Shrew beckoned them toward the door at the end of the corridor.

Carthinal followed and found himself in a large room. Several small tables were scattered around with a few people sitting at them. Some played Rond, a card game popular on Vimar, while others sat around talking or mending clothes and tools.

Light streamed in through two large windows opposite

the door. As with everything else, they were clean and polished. A large table stood under one of the windows, and a man sat on an oversized chair behind it.

He stood as the three entered the room. He wore a tunic of red and blue with green trousers. His hair, which had been dyed red, stood up, making a line of hair from front to back. His long nose led as he craned his neck forward to look at them.

"What's this you've brought?"

"We found 'im. Bleedin' Green Fish attacked 'im," the boy known as Cat replied. "Well, a couple of 'em, anyway. They was on our patch, so we saw 'em off."

"Why bring 'im 'ere? 'E looks like one o' them rich bods."

"'E were, but 'e were cheated of 'is 'ouse, 'e sez."

Rooster rounded the table and walked around Carthinal, looking him up and down. Carthinal shuffled his feet as he watched the man.

Italics, but not bold.He does look like a rooster, with his hair sticking up like that. It's just like a cock's comb. He even walks like a rooster. And his nose is like a beak.

Rooster returned to face Carthinal again. "Cat says you might want t'join us. What d'you say?"

Carthinal looked around the room. All eyes turned in his direction, and a few people left their places and now stood in a circle, looking at him. He looked at the ground.

Turning his eyes to the person referred to as Cat, he said, "I never said that!"

The small, dark-haired boy grinned. "Not in so many words, no. But you was on our patch. You'll be stealin' soon. You steal on our patch, you better be in the Beasts or we'll deal wi' you like we did Green Fish."

"Who says I'll steal? Stealing's wrong."

Rooster looked hard at Carthinal through narrowed eyes.

"'Ow much money 'ave you, boy? You say you got no 'ome. Your money'll run out soon if that's true. Then you'll steal to live. You can join us or not. Up to you, but if you don't, expect us to sort you out like Cat and Bull sorted Green Fish. You'll not survive long. Green Fish'll be after you, too. You join the Beasts and we'll give you food, protection and a 'ome."

Carthinal stood looking at the young man in front of him. What he said was true. He closed his eyes as he thought.

"Oh, I forgot to tell you," Rooster interrupted his thoughts. "We 'old everythin' in common. You 'ave to give us what you 'ave."

Carthinal stepped back. "I only have a little money left. You can't take that."

Rooster shrugged. "'Ave it your own way." He turned to go back to his chair. Then he stopped and looked back at Carthinal. "We'll get th' money anyway. One of us'll catch you and take it. Pr'ob'ly beat you a bit, too, 'cos you'll be stealin', or beggin', on our patch, see. So you lose it anyway."

Carthinal felt in his pocket. He gripped his few royals tightly. What were his choices? No doubt he would be robbed sooner or later. Green Fish had already tried. And the money wouldn't last forever. What would he do then?

He did not like the idea of joining a street gang, but what choice did he have? He pulled his hand from his pocket and handed his coins to Rooster.

"Sensible lad." Rooster took the money and called to a young man sitting by the window. "Tiger, bring th' money pot. We've a bit more ter put in it." He peered at the three royals in his hand. "Precious little, but it's better'n nowt."

Tiger lifted a pot from one of the shelves and carried it carefully over to Rooster. Carthinal watched his last few coins disappear into the pot and sighed. No turning back now.

"You need a name," one of the girls called out.

"I'm called Carthinal."

"No, a gang name. We don't use our given names 'ere. As we're the Beasts, we all 'ave animal names. I'm Porcupine."

Another boy chimed up, "I know. 'E's got red 'air. 'E can be Fox."

CHAPTER THREE

CARTHINAL SPENT THE NEXT FEW MONTHS MASTERING the language of the underworld. Rooster would not allow him to leave the headquarters until he was proficient. He must be able to talk with other members of the gang without the guards understanding.

One day, after he had been with the Beasts for six months, Rooster called to him. "Fox, you go with Wren. There'll be lots of punters out in the market. They'll be preparing for the feast of Bramara on the winter solstice. She'll pick a pocket, then pass it to you. You leave in the opposite direction an' come back 'ere. Don't run. That'd raise suspicions."

Carthinal grinned. At last, Rooster trusted him to do a job. His eyes glowed with an inner light, and he jigged on the spot.

"Fox," Rooster called as they passed him. "Cover yer 'ead. Yer auburn 'air is too distinctive. Can't do anythin' 'bout those eyes, but don't look straight at anyone. No one else 'as eyes that dark blue."

Carthinal nodded as he pulled the hood of his cloak over his hair and left in the company of Wren.

Wren had brown hair and eyes and was of small stature as

befitted her name as the small bird. They walked to the market, but as soon as they entered, Wren whispered to Carthinal.

"We separate 'ere. Keep me in sight. When you see me bump into a punter, come to me. Don't stop. I'll put the stuff into yer 'and. Keep on goin' and don't look at me."

Carthinal mingled with the crowds, pretending to look at the goods in the market, always keeping Wren in sight. She passed many people, and Carthinal wondered how she chose her victim. He saw her stumble and bump into a rich-looking woman.

He strode toward her and heard her say, "I'm sorry, ma'am. Caught me foot on summat." She looked down as if to search for what had tripped her.

Carthinal walked by, close to the woman and Wren and felt her hand touch his. He gripped something and continued walking, stuffing it into his pocket as he went. After a few yards, he turned in the direction of the gang's headquarters.

Wren caught up with him. "Well done. You're a natural."

"I did all right, then?" He grinned.

"Very good for a first time. In fact, I've 'ad buddies wors'n that after years o' practice."

Carthinal puffed his chest out. He would make sure he was the best in the gang.

When they got back to the headquarters, Rooster patted them both on the back. "Looks like you'll make a good pair. A good 'aul 'ere, too. There's even an emperor in the purse."

He held up a large coin made of platinum. "A few copper royals, ten silver crowns, and three gold monarchs as well." He grinned and sent them for some food at the opposite end of the large room.

* * *

Carthinal had been sharing a room with Cat who hoped to be a cat burglar and had begun his training. Before long, he and Carthinal became firm friends.

"What do yer want to do, 'ere?" Cat queried one day.

Carthinal shrugged. "Not sure."

"How d'yer fancy bein' a burglar? Lots of excitement."

"No, that doesn't appeal to me."

"Y' could be a pick-pocket, like Wren, or Rooster could set yer up in a shop in town, an' you could be a fence." Cat scanned Carthinal from head to foot. "I don't think you'd be very good as security, though. We need people built like Bull for that. Then there're th' beggars. They play on people's sympathy. Usually with an injury or summat. You ain't got no damn injury, but you're bloody pretty enough to make punters feel sorry for yer."

"I've not thought about it, Cat. I suppose I should."

It was decided for him, eventually.

Rooster called him one day. "Fox, yer must earn yer keep. We ain't a charity. Go over to Snake an' say I told 'im ter teach yer 'ow ter pick a pocket. Yer did well when you went out wi' Wren that time, but now it's time for you to learn to be the dip."

Carthinal began to learn the art of picking pockets under Snake's tutelage. Snake, as his name implies, was a slippery customer. He was tall and slender with thin, brown hair and green eyes.

"Fox, I 'ave a pouch in me pocket. I'm gonna walk over there." He pointed to the opposite side of the room. "I want yer t' get it out of me pocket. Dunna worry 'bout me feelin' yer at th' moment. Just get it."

This Carthinal did. In spite of what Snake said, he tried to get it without the young man feeling him.

"Not bad. Yer technique's not quite right, but we'll work on that. Yer did well for a first time."

* * *

Over the next few months, Carthinal became better at picking pockets.

One day Rooster called him over. "Snake tells me you're ready to go with Wren. This time you are to be the 'dip' while she receives the goods."

The pair arrived at the market, and Carthinal noticed a man with a bulging pocket. He walked towards him, looking the other way, then stumbled and bumped into the man. He slipped his hand into the man's pocket and extracted a full purse. Wren walked past as if she were looking at the stall, and Carthinal pressed the purse into her hand then walked in the opposite direction.

The victim put his hand to his pocket to get his money to pay for a purchase. "Hey, I've been robbed." He scanned the marketplace. Turning to the man next to him, he said, "Did you see anything?"

The man shook his head.

Carthinal looked back and heard this exchange but continued wending his way towards the gang's headquarters. No one noticed the boy weaving between them. They were more interested in what was going on at the stall, where the victim stridently called for the Guard.

Back at the headquarters, Wren handed the pouch over to Rooster.

"Well done, the pair of you. Fox, you're proving yourself a 'andy pickpocket."

* * *

Several months later, as Carthinal and Wren were leaving on a job, Bull charged into the headquarters.

"Bleedin' Green Fish on our patch." He bent over as he paused for breath. "Their bloody boss is wi' 'em, too. I think they want ter try a take-over."

Rooster surged to his feet and began pointing and giving orders. "Fox, Wren, come 'ere. Job's cancelled. Porcupine, get th' weapons. Bull, find th' other big guys and come back 'ere. Quickly. Everyone gather round."

Porcupine arrived pulling a large chest. Rooster opened it and began handing out weapons. Daggers in the main, but he gave bows to a couple of the stronger lads, who set about stringing them. Carthinal watched as they heaved on the heavy wood, realising the bows would need a great deal of strength to draw.

"Fox, take this knife."

"I've never used one before." Carthinal looked at the weapon, turning it over in his hands.

"Mind." Wren came up and took it from him. "It's sharp. Very. You c'd cut yer fingers off."

Carthinal grimaced and retrieved it from her. "I'll be careful. What happens now?"

"We go and fight Green Fish off our patch."

Carthinal frowned and looked at his knife again. "I don't know how to fight."

It was Wren's turn to grimace. "Then you'll 'ave ter learn quick. That or die." She gave a little laugh. "I'd 'ate ter see that 'appen."

The gang was making its way through the door and into the street. Wren and Carthinal rushed to catch up. Green Fish had set themselves up in the park where Carthinal had slept when he first found himself on the streets, and where the two boys from Green Fish had tried to rob him. The opposing gang, about thirty strong, stood in the entrance to the park.

A few citizens were out strolling as it was a pleasant spring day—one of the first of the year. They stopped, frozen in their tracks.

Rooster stepped in front of the rest of the gang. "You're on our patch."

Another young man stepped in front of the group facing the Beasts. "Sez 'oo?"

"Sez me, and we're gonna see you gone or dead."

He beckoned the rest of the gang, who rushed through the gates. As soon as the gate cleared, the citizens rushed out, anxious to be as far away from this trouble as possible. Carthinal watched them go, wishing he could go with them, but he must fight. How should he do it?

"Come on," Wren whispered. "We're missing all the fun."

Italics, but not bold.Fun? What's fun about getting hurt, or possibly getting killed? In spite of his fears, Carthinal rushed towards the fight, after Wren.

It looked like chaos to Carthinal. He grasped his knife, trying to find someone whom he didn't know to stab. He looked around. He recognised everyone. All the people near him were part of the Beasts.

Looking around in the chaos, he saw someone he knew. Someone who was not one of the Beasts. Someone who had tried to rob him.

He felt his anger rise from somewhere in his stomach. Carthinal deserved to have his own back on this young man, and, although smaller, he rushed through the melee. He almost tripped over a body lying on the ground but managed to catch his balance. The stumble propelled him toward his selected victim. He held his knife before him and thrust it forward.

The young man in question had his back to Carthinal. The dagger entered between his ribs and pierced a lung. He went down with a cry. Carthinal smiled.

He found himself in the middle of the battle. How dare these people try to take over his gang's territory? His anger had not been assuaged. The stabbing of his enemy only fed it. He swung the knife at random and made contact with a young woman's eyes. She screamed and fell.

It went on for what seemed like hours to Carthinal. When the last of Green Fish ran away, leaving their friends groaning on the park grass, he looked at the sky. The sun had not moved far. The battle had taken no more than half an hour. He looked around to see how many of his friends had been injured.

There was Rooster, covered in blood, but checking those lying on the ground. Some he helped to their feet, calling others to take them away. Some he sighed over, bent and closed their eyes, but most he left.

The sound of pounding feet brought Carthinal to his senses. Cat, blood running from a cut on his cheek, called, "Run! It's the Guard. If they catch you, you might as well 'ave been killed 'ere."

Those who could scattered in all directions. The guards tried to pursue them but lost them as soon as they got into the poor quarter and the warren of streets that made up that area.

Gradually all the Beasts made their way back to head-quarters.

Rooster counted them. "We lost five. I 'ope the injured make it back. I sent 'em off wi' 'elp afore the guards arrived."

Slowly, the injured, and those helping them, returned.

"Did we lose any on the way?" Rooster asked Scorpion, who was helping the injured.

"No. We all got back."

Carthinal looked around the room. Some had minor wounds, others more serious. He had a cut on his hand, and one young woman had managed to cut his shirt, but the knife had not cut flesh.

"Where's Wren?" He felt a hollow feeling in his stomach as he realised she was nowhere to be seen. He scanned the room again, beginning to feel a little light-headed as he could not see her anywhere. He hugged himself as panic began to rise.

Rooster scanned the room. He turned to Scorpion. "We didn't all get back. Wren isn't 'ere."

Scorpion hung his head. "Sorry, boss. I thought she were wi' Fox."

"Kassilla's tits. Thought? Thought?" Rooster paced up and down. "What do you mean, 'Thought'? Did you think to check with Fox?"

Scorpion shook his head. "Sorry," he repeated, shuffling his feet.

"We must find her." Rooster began organising the search. "She wasn't among the dead, so she left the park. Let's hope she's not been caught by the bloody Guard."

Carthinal turned away with Cat to search. "I think th' Guard did catch 'er," Cat said. "I 'ope not. Th' penalty fer killin' is death by 'angin'."

"But we don't know that she killed anyone."

"There were a fight. Folks got killed. She were in the fight, so they'll blame 'er fer killin'."

Carthinal frowned, a sadness filling his indigo eyes. "Come on. The first place to look is the jail."

"We can't go ter th' jail, Fox. They'll 'ave us in there as soon as we appear."

"Do you want to find Wren? If not, I'll go myself."

"Nah! I'm comin' wi' yer. I'm usually a lucky bloke. You

have luck too, Fox. Mayhap our combined luck'll 'elp us find Wren."

Rooster, who had sat on his chair, head in his hands, looked up.

"You're right." He looked around at the rest of the gang, some of whom had paled at the thought of Wren in the hands of the Guard. "Someone must rescue 'er. We can't leave 'er there to be executed. We can't storm the bleedin' jail. It'll be better if only you two go." He stood and ran his hands through his hair. "Bring her back safely."

CHAPTER FOUR

THE PAIR LEFT THE POOR QUARTER AND PASSED THROUGH the market square. People stood around gossiping about the fight that had taken place in the park. As the two neared the jail, they paused.

The jail stood at one end of the market place. A solid building, it had a wide door in the centre with barred windows to either side. Carthinal had seen it often, but it had never appeared so intimidating as it did now.

"I'll climb onto th' roof an' see if I can find anythin' out. There's a chimney I can listen at." Cat sprinted around the side of the jailhouse and began to climb. Carthinal hid in a doorway opposite, chewing his fingernails.

Soon, Cat returned. "They've got 'er, alright. They've got a couple o' the bleedin' Green Fish, too. Put 'em in th' same damned cell, they 'ave. By luck, th' blasted Green Fish 'aven't started on 'er. Not yet, any'ow."

"How can we rescue her without the Green Fish escaping, too? In fact, how can we rescue her at all?"

Cat thought for a moment. "If we can some'ow get th'

bleedin' guards out o' there, I can slip in an' pick th' lock. 'Ow t'stop th' blasted Green Fish gettin' out, too, I've no idea."

Carthinal pressed his lips together as he walked towards the jailhouse. He must rescue Wren. She was his partner, yes, but more than that.

Italic, but not bold. He chewed on his lip. I must rescue her. She makes me feel good. My heart beats fast when I touch her. I can't let her be executed, no matter what.

He passed through the door and found himself in a single room. On his left were two cells, and a table stood immediately in front of him. A guard leant back on two legs of the chair with his feet propped on the table. He had his eyes closed. Carthinal drew in a breath. It was the guard who had thrown him out of Gromblo's offices.

He turned to make a rude comment to get the guard to chase him but he heard a voice.

"Fox!"

The voice came from the second of the two cells. Carthinal looked and saw a pair of hands gripping the bars of the door.

At the sound of her voice, the guard opened his eyes. "It's you! Kendo Brolin's grandson. What are you doing here?"

Carthinal swallowed the words he was about to say and looked at the guard with eyes wide. "You believe I'm his grandson?"

The guard nodded. "There was something funny about that death certificate. And there ain't too many red-headed half-elf kids about."

"Then why didn't you help me? Why didn't you expose him?"

"Grondin has friends in high places. It would have been dangerous to try. Besides, he made it worth my while to keep quiet." He swung his feet down. "How come you know this girl? She called you Fox. Are you with the Beasts now?"

Carthinal glanced towards the cell door and did not answer.

"You know there's a warrant out for the Beasts and Green Fish?"

Wren called out from her cell. "There's always a warrant for us. What's new?"

The guard stood and walked towards the cell. "You keep out of this. There'll be a rope for you."

Carthinal thought quickly. How could he get the guard to release Wren? He had an idea.

"You said you knew the death certificate Gromblo showed you was forged. That means you knew he swindled me out of my inheritance, yet you did nothing. You took his bribe and left me to starve on the streets. I was lucky enough to fall in with the Beasts and that's kept me alive."

The guard looked at him through narrowed eyes. "What are you saying, boy?"

"I'm saying it would be hard on you if your superiors found out. Even after a year, they'd still not take a good view of a guard taking a bribe."

"You go to the bosses and they'll arrest you before you get one word out." He smirked at Carthinal.

"But if they got a letter, they wouldn't know who it came from, would they? They'd have to investigate, and you would be dismissed. What would you do then?"

The guard laughed. "And who'll write a letter? You street kids are illiterate."

"Are you so sure about that? Aren't you forgetting who my grandfather was? He sent me to school."

The guard blanched. "What do you want?"

"I want my friend released."

"And how will I explain where she's gone?"

"You'll think of something. Now, give me the keys, and you stop those Green Fish from breaking out when I unlock the door."

The guard picked up the keys, but before handing them to Carthinal, he turned toward the main door.

Carthinal jumped in front of him and drew his knife. His nostrils flared and his eyes blazed "Oh no you don't! You're not going to run out on me."

The guard put up his hands. "I'm just going to lock this door, then if those thugs make a run for it they can't get out. I'll get them back into their cage then unlock the door for you and your friend."

Watching closely, Carthinal held onto his knife and kept it pointed at the guard's throat as he locked the jailhouse door and went to unlock the cell.

Wren rushed out, followed by the two Green Fish. The guard tackled one of them, bringing him tumbling to the ground. The youth rolled over on top of the guard and looked like being able to overpower him, but the guard bucked and threw him off. As luck would have it, the prisoner banged his head on the wall of the cell and lay still.

Carthinal and Wren took on the other youth. He was a big young man, but Carthinal threatened him with his knife. As the Green Fish man approached, Wren stuck out her foot and gave him a push. He stumbled enough for Carthinal to finish his fall and sit on top of him.

He held the Green Fish's long hair and pulled back, holding his knife at the other's throat. "Now go back into your cell like a good boy," Carthinal said with a smirk, "or I might forget I'm a nice person."

31

The guard dragged the first youth into the cell, and the second went in quietly, looking all the time at Carthinal. "They'll end up on the hangman's gibbet, no doubt. Now get out of here before I have second thoughts."

Carthinal grinned. "You won't. I know too much about you."

He and Wren left the jailhouse and met Cat outside. "Kassilla's tits, what kept you? I thought you were goin' in ter lure th' guy out."

"Long story, Cat, but I found a better way to do it. I'll tell you on the way back to HQ."

Wren reached up and kissed Carthinal on the cheek. "Thank you for rescuing me."

He blushed and felt as if all the butterflies in the world had taken residence in his stomach. "I...it was nothing. You're my partner."

Wren smiled.

* * *

Another year passed. Carthinal had been with the Beasts for over two years. There had been many more fights like the one with Green Fish. Other gangs tried to take over the Beasts' territory. It was the best territory in Bluehaven, having the market as part of it. Carthinal learned to fight with his knife and usually came away with few injuries.

"The luck of the elves," Wren told him.

His relationship with Wren deepened, and soon they shared a room. They were a good team, too, and Rooster was proud of the way they always got a good haul when they went out to pickpockets.

It was the spring equinox, Grillon's Day, and the first day of spring. Grillon's Day was a day of celebration all over Grosmer. Grillon was the god of the wild and wild creatures and the patron of hunters, but everyone worshipped him on this day. All except the gangs.

Carthinal and Wren went to the stone circle outside the city. Not to worship the god, but because it would be a good place to pickpockets.

They were not the only people from the underworld there. Religious celebrations always brought out the beggars. Carthinal noticed several of the Beasts' beggars amongst those sitting outside the circle.

There were three circles outside Bluehaven and Rooster had sent Carthinal and Wren to the western one. The pair mingled with the worshippers entering the circle. Wren picked pockets and passed her gains to Carthinal, who slipped away unnoticed before the priest arrived to accept the gifts for sacrifice.

After the services, people came into the towns to feast and be entertained, then in the evening, there was dancing around the bonfires, after which couples sneaked away into the woods. They considered any children born after this celebration as Grillon's legitimate children.

After the religious ceremony, and a night of love, the people made their way to the city's main square. This year, the town council had billed a magician to appear, and Carthinal and Wren got to the square early. They stood hand in hand waiting for the show to begin.

It began with dancers in the centre of the square, then a group of singers appeared. Clowns and people on stilts followed. The stilt walkers danced and the audience clapped, cheered and threw money into the arena. A man dressed in a clown's costume went round with a bucket, picking the coins up. After he had picked all those on the ground, he went around the crowd, shaking it for people to add more.

A woman brought her dogs into the square and they ran around seemingly at random. She pulled a flute from a pocket and began to play and dance. The dogs followed her movements and soon they were all dancing, weaving around each other. That brought more cheers, and people threw money again. The same clown picked it up and asked for more from the crowd.

Finally, the magician appeared wearing a deep blue robe with stars and moons printed all over it. The robe had a hood, which the magician wore pulled up over his head so no one could see his face. He waved his hands around and pulled coins out of the air.

"I wish I could do that," Wren whispered. "We'd no longer have to steal to make a living. We'd be rich."

"I don't think it's real magic, though," Carthinal replied. "If he could conjure coins, I don't think he'd be here doing that."

The magician approached the crowd where he reached out and pulled a sweetmeat from behind a small boy's ear. He handed it to the child who put it in his mouth and grinned.

This went on for some time until Carthinal felt a prickling all over his skin. He scratched.

"What's wrong?" Wren asked. "Got fleas?"

Carthinal shook his head and watched the magician carefully. He was muttering some words and a flame appeared on one of his fingers. Still muttering, he made it jump from one finger to the next.

For the next few tricks, Carthinal felt nothing, and then he felt the tingling again. It was as though tiny mice were running up and down his arms, digging their little claws into him. A shiver ran down his spine.

The magician held a globe of light that changed colour as he moved it around. He threw it into the air and it turned blue, then disappeared against the sky.

This went on for some time. The crowd loved it, especially when the magician conjured bursts of coloured lights in the sky. All this time, Carthinal's skin prickled.

After the show, as the pair walked back to the headquarters, Carthinal said, "I think some of that was real magic. Not all of it, of course, just some of it."

"What makes you say that?"

"Didn't you get a prickling of your skin when he did certain things?"

Wren shook her head. "No, Nothing. Why?"

Carthinal looked down at her. "Doesn't matter. I thought it was interesting, that's all."

The magician performed in the square for several days. Each day, Carthinal went and watched. By the sensation of pins and needles, he learned which of the man's tricks were real magic and which sleight of hand.

Wren went with him the first couple of times, then she said, "Why do you keep going back? It's the same show every day."

Carthinal shrugged. "I'm unsure myself, Wren. I'm fascinated by his magic. His real magic, that is, not that other stuff."

After watching many times, Carthinal thought he could remember the words and hand movements the magician made when he conjured the small flame on his finger. He decided to try it out, but not in the gang's headquarters.

He walked around the area until he came to a back street. Sitting on a doorstep, he began to mutter the words and copy what he thought were the hand movements. Nothing happened. He tried again. Still nothing. After a few attempts, he gave up.

The next day, he was again standing in the square watching. He thought he noticed a few things he'd got wrong, and he went to practise again, in the same back street.

He practised for a week. By then, the magician had left the area.

One day, sitting on the step, he wondered why he did this. The man he had been copying had gone, so he could not refresh his memory. He sat there, head in his hands, trying to picture exactly what the magician had said and done.

I'll try one more time. If it doesn't work, I'll give up.

He chanted the words in a slightly different way. His skin began to prickle and he felt a sensation deep within his stomach. Tension built up inside him then suddenly released as a tiny flame appeared on his index finger, then vanished.

The young man leapt up and yelled. "Yay! I did it!"

He ran all the way back to headquarters and burst in shouting, "Wren, Wren, I did it!"

"Calm down. Did what?"

"Made magic. I got a little flame on my finger."

Wren shrugged. "So what? How's that going to help with anything?"

Carthinal took her by her shoulders. "Don't you see? I can do magic. Perhaps if I practise, I can learn more and then perform like that magician. We could be rich."

"Who's goin' ter be rich?" Cat was passing.

"Cat, I managed to do some magic. Real magic."

Cat laughed. "You think 'cos yer did a little bleedin' trick yer can become a real mage? Dream on, Fox, but keep 'em for sleep-time."

Carthinal shook his head but determined to keep on practising. Apart from the pride in learning to do it all on his own, when he had succeeded, the physical sensations it gave him were enough to make him continue. He thought about the gradual build-up and sudden release, and the ecstasy he felt when it happened. He wanted that again. But could he repeat it?

CHAPTER FIVE

EACH MORNING, CARTHINAL WENT TO THE SAME BACK street, chanted and wove his hands around. Sometimes he succeeded, sometimes he failed, but he did not give up. Eventually, he could keep the flame going for several minutes.

One day, as he tried to make the flame walk from one finger to another, a shadow fell over him. Quickly, he extinguished his little flame and sprang to his feet.

"Steady, lad," a voice said. "How did you learn to do that?"

Carthinal looked the man up and down. He wore a black robe, indicating he was a mage, and had dark hair and blue eyes.

Carthinal scowled. "Why should I tell you? Who are you, and how did you find me?"

"My name's Mabryl. I'm an archmage and I felt a disturbance in the mana, so I tracked it here."

At the sound of "archmage," Carthinal pricked up his ears. "Archmage? You're important, then. So why've you tracked me down?"

"One simple reason. Hardly anyone can learn to do magic of any kind on their own. What made you try?"

"I watched the magician in the square on Grillon's Day and during that week. I copied what he said and did."

"Impressive. How did you know what to copy? How did you know what was real magic and what wasn't?'

"I felt it. It was like a tingling all over my skin."

The archmage's eyes widened. "Young man, you have a great talent for magic, but you need training. First, although you've managed to get this far on your own, that's only a very simple spell. One we use to teach apprentices at the beginning. It's called a cantrip. More importantly, though, is the fact that magic can be very dangerous in untrained hands, both to yourself and those around you."

Carthinal looked into Archmage Mabryl's eyes. "What are you saying? I should stop?"

"Not at all. You have a tremendous talent. I would like to train you."

"No. I'll not fall for that. You know who I am and want to lure me to your home so you can hand me over to the guards."

Mabryl laughed a soft laugh. "Not at all. That would be such a waste of talent. Anyway, who are you that I'd want to hand you over? What have you done that the guards would be interested in?"

Carthinal looked down and shuffled his feet. "Nothing. At least nothing you need to know. I need to go."

As he turned to leave, Mabryl said, "I live on Grindlehoff Street. Number forty-three. Come there if you change your mind. I hope you do. Your talent will be wasted if not, and you could cause great danger to everyone around."

When Carthinal got back to the headquarters, he searched out Wren and told her all that had happened.

"What did you say?"

"I told him he could go away and leave me alone. I'm not interested. He's only trying to tempt me so I'll lead him to the rest of you."

That night, Wren propped herself up on her elbow on the bed they shared. "I've been thinkin'."

"Not too hard. I hope." Carthinal yawned and turned to face her.

"About that man, Mabryl, was it?"

"What about him?"

"If you went there and learned to be a proper mage, you could be a 'elp to the gang."

"How?"

"Suppose you could use magic to 'elp people not notice us when we pick their pockets? Then p'rhaps you c'd make Cat invisible when 'e goes buglarin' so's no one sees 'im. Or you could use it when we fight other gangs. We'd be able to take over all the others."

"Mmm. Perhaps. I'll think about it." He turned over and went to sleep.

Carthinal changed the spot where Archmage Mabryl found him, deciding he would be safer elsewhere. Even so, a nagging thought dogged him. Would Mabryl be able to find him in the same way he had previously?

He did not want to become part of the established society. Ever since the theft of his inheritance, he had felt apart from it. The Beasts had become his family. They had been good to him. So what if it involved criminal activity and possibly killing or being killed in a fight? He had a home and friends, and a lovely girlfriend.

He sat in some shrubs practising his magic spell. Sometimes it worked and sometimes it did not, though it was beginning to work more often than it failed.

Mabryl found him again, of course. "I see you've made progress. Are you sure you don't want to learn more? How are you going to learn more spells?"

"Go away. I don't want your help."

Mabryl raised an eyebrow. "Really? As I said—how are you going to learn to do more spells?"

"My friend will come and steal a spellbook. I know you mages have books with your spells written in them."

"Perhaps the books are trapped with magic. What then?"

"Oh, go away!" Carthinal shouted as he jumped to his feet. "I don't want to come to your house. I'll find a way to learn. Just leave me alone." He turned and ran back to the headquarters of the Beasts.

Three weeks passed and life continued as normal. Carthinal had to go out picking pockets with Wren. Cat continued to improve his burglary skills and Bull had grown into an impressively muscular young man in the two years Carthinal had been with the Beasts. He now ran the security of the gang.

Carthinal was sitting watching four of the gang playing a game of Rond, a card game popular in Grosmer, when Rooster called him. "Fox, I believe you've 'ad an offer ter learn magic."

Carthinal puckered his brows. "Who told you?"

"Wren, o' course. 'Oo else? She also told me 'ow useful she thinks magic might be in the gang. I agree. I think yer should take this man's offer."

"No!"

"You should go and learn, then come back 'ere to us." Rooster continued as if Carthinal had not spoken.

"I said no!"

Rooster walked away shrugging his shoulders and said no more of it, but Carthinal did not forget about the feeling when he managed to conjure the tiny flame. He craved the power of a mage.

One afternoon, he found himself standing opposite Mabryl's house. He stood there for an hour, looking.

The house was a modest one by the standard of his grandfather's house but was not one of someone of little means. The front door sported a porch between two sets of windows. There were windows above them as well as one over the porch, though it had no third storey like his grandfather's house and no basement. He took a couple of steps toward the door, but, like a young fawn confronted by a wolf, he turned and fled.

He returned three days in a row, but each time lost his nerve. On the fourth day, he mustered up the courage to knock.

There came the sound of footsteps and the door slowly opened. A woman in her mid-forties stood there, dark hair peppered with grey. Her light blue eyes narrowed as she, frowned when she saw him. "What do you want? We need no beggars here. Be off with you!"

She went to close the door.

"I want to speak with Archmage Mabryl."

Her frown deepened. "What does the likes of you want with a respected archmage? He doesn't want to see you. Go away."

Carthinal heard heavy footsteps approaching, then a familiar voice saying, "What is it Lillora?"

She turned and spoke to Mabryl. "A young man, fourteen or fifteen by the looks of him. He says he wants to speak with you. I told him to go away. He looks dirty and untidy."

"Ah! I know who it is. Let him in. I've been expecting him."

The door opened wider to reveal a hallway with stairs on the left-hand side.

"Come in." Mabryl beckoned as the young man continued to stand at the threshold. "Come into my study and we can talk."

With faltering steps, Carthinal entered the house. He followed Mabryl into a room on the left.

The young man stopped as he entered and gazed around him. The room was a treasure trove. Two large windows faced the street with a floor to ceiling wooden bookcase between them. Opposite the windows was a fireplace with shelves filling the spaces on either side. On the shelves were bottles and jars filled with things Carthinal could not name.

A large table stood in the centre of the room. Books covered that, too. He had never seen so many books in one place before. No, that was not right. He'd never seen so many books in his entire life.

Sitting at one end of the table, a young girl of about twelve or thirteen looked up as he and Mabryl entered. Carthinal appraised her. She had brown hair, eyes a shade lighter, and a rather plain face.

"You said you can read." Mabryl walked over to the bookshelf and searched through the books before pulling one from the shelf. He walked over to Carthinal and handed it to him. "Read me some of this."

Carthinal turned the book over in his hands. He read the title, *History of the Forbidding,* and opened it at random. He began reading aloud.

"The mage war ended eventu...eventually, but it had taken a great toll on the inno...cent. Innocent." He glanced up. Mabryl looked at him intently.

He continued reading. "King Consyl the Third was deter...determin...determined?" He looked at Mabryl, who nodded. Carthinal continued. "Determined such a war would not happen again. He forbade the practice of magic on pain of death. All spellbooks, he... decreed, must be burned."

"That will do," Mabryl told him. "You can indeed read, even if it needs some polishing. Now, about writing. Let's see how you do at that. Copy out what you've just read on this sheet of paper. You'll find ink and a pen on the desk."

Carthinal sat in the chair, picked up the pen and began to copy the passage, frowning all the time. His tongue stuck out at the side of his mouth as he concentrated. He had not written anything in the time he had been with the Beasts. He dropped a few spots of ink on the paper and scowled. Mabryl would never want him as an apprentice if he made a mess of this.

"That'll do." Mabryl came over and peered at what Carthinal had done. "A bit messy, but precision will come with practice. Is there anything you need to go and get? I'll show you where you'll be sleeping."

Carthinal's eyes widened. "Sleeping? I'll be sleeping here?"

"Yes, of course. Apprentices always stay with their master. Follow me." He walked through the door, leaving Carthinal with no choice but to follow him.

They ascended the stairs onto a landing. Mabryl led Carthinal to a door on the left. He opened it and stood back for Carthinal to enter.

The room was large enough to have two beds, with a wardrobe and chest.

"This is where you'll sleep. Lillora will buy you some clothes. Those you've got on need to be burned by the look of them. You will also bathe. There's a copper for heating water downstairs. I'm not having you sleeping in my beds as you are. You've probably got fleas or something." He said this as he watched Carthinal scratch his head.

"And one thing you've not told me."

Carthinal looked puzzled. What now?

Mabryl smiled. "If you are going to be my apprentice, I need to know your name."

Carthinal's face showed relief. Mabryl did not want to know about his crimes. "It's Carthinal, sir."

"Good. Now we know each other. Go and get that bath." Mabryl turned and left the room.

Carthinal did as he was asked, and while he sat waiting for the water to heat up in the copper urn, Lillora went to buy some clothes.

Once the water was hot, Carthinal took a bucket and poured water into a metal tub. He climbed in and soaked himself, then plastered soap all over his body. Especially his hair. Mabryl had been right. He probably did have fleas.

As he lay in the hot water, enjoying the sensation, his thoughts turned to the gang. Rooster had told him to come and learn magic. Did he know that Carthinal would have to stay with Mabryl? How would he get a message to Wren to let her know? Would she think he'd abandoned her?

Lillora returned with the clothes, leaving them outside the door. She knocked to let him know, and Carthinal climbed out of the tub, dried himself and dressed. Lillora had bought him a pair of brown trousers, tunic and a grey shirt. He felt better than he had in a long time. He had forgotten what it was like to be clean.

Carthinal left the bathhouse through the door to the kitchen. As he entered the room, Lillora was carrying some plates through to the dining room.

She stopped and looked at him. "That's better. You look

almost presentable now. Come on through to dinner." She paused and looked at his shoulder-length auburn hair. "I'd get that cut, if I were you. You'd look better with it shorter."

Carthinal pressed his lips together. *Not now you've told me, I won't.*

CHAPTER SIX

A FEW NIGHTS LATER, AS SOON AS DARKNESS FELL, Carthinal looked out of his window. Could he climb out and go back to the Beasts? They would need to know what had happened to him. Yes. A tree grew outside. It would be a risk, but he thought he could probably manage to reach the nearest branch.

Climbing onto the windowsill, Carthinal reached out but wobbled dangerously. Steadying himself, he tried again and managed to grab a small branch. He pulled it towards him and soon found he could reach a larger one.

He took a deep breath and, hanging onto the large branch, he leapt from his window. Fortunately, the branch held and he shimmied along it to the main trunk where he climbed down. He looked up at his window. How am I going to get back in? He shrugged. That was a question for later. He trotted off towards his gang's headquarters.

"Fox!" Wren yelled as he entered the gang's headquarters. She rushed over and threw her arms around him, ignoring the looks from others in the room. "What happened? Did that mage let you in? Are you going to learn magic?"

He hugged her back and grinned as he kissed her. "Yes, Mabryl has accepted me as an apprentice. I'll be learning magic."

Wren took his arm and led him to a chair in the corner where they could have a bit of privacy in the busy room. She kissed him and sat on his lap. "What have you learned so far?"

Carthinal's grin disappeared, and his brows furrowed. "Nothing, yet. Not even how to get that little flame every time. Mabryl says I'm too ill-disciplined and that magic needs concentration. Apparently, I'm not able to concentrate well enough to learn any spells safely."

"You've got new clothes. And you're clean. You smell good. Come on, let's go to our room."

But that had to wait as Rooster strode toward them. "Fox, 'ow's it goin'?" He shook Carthinal's hand.

"It'll take some time. Magic's difficult to learn. Harder than picking pockets."

"Well, we can wait. Time's something we've plenty of. As long as we get the upper 'and an' become the leadin' gang in town, then we can wait." He strode away to talk to Bull and Ox who were practising wrestling.

Carthinal and Wren whispered in their chair until Wren pulled him up. "We need more privacy, Fox. Let's go to my room."

The pair climbed the stairs at the back of the room and entered the third door on the right.

The room had four beds, all neatly made with a trunk at the bottom of each. Wren led him past the first bed to one under the window and pulled him down onto it.

She kissed him passionately. "Oh, 'ow I missed you." She ran her fingers through his shoulder-length auburn hair that had given him his gang name of Fox. "I'm glad they 'aven't made you cut yer 'air."

Carthinal laughed. "Lillora, the housekeeper, said I should cut it." He looked around the room. "Who else sleeps in here, and won't they want to come to bed at some time?"

"When they saw you, they all gave me a little nod. They'll find somewhere else to sleep tonight. We 'ave it all to ourselves."

She lay back on the bed and Carthinal looked at her. What a beautiful girl. And talented. Our best dip. I'm so lucky. He leaned over and kissed her again before beginning to remove her clothes.

They continued their lovemaking. They did not hear footsteps pass the door as others found their beds, nor the giggles as Wren's roommates listened at the door. They only had eyes and ears for each other.

As they lay naked on the bed, Carthinal said, "I should get back. No one knows I'm out."

Wren kissed him again. "Not yet. There's plenty of time. Tell me about Mabryl and what it's like livin' there. 'Ow much 'ave you learned? When'll you start doing real magic? 'Ow long does it take to become a real mage?"

"Whoa! One question at a time."

Carthinal began to tell her about what he had been doing while living with Mabryl. After a few minutes, he kissed her again. "I can think of better things to do than talk about Mabryl."

He shivered as Wren ran her hands down his back and his body responded to her actions. He stroked her hair, then her neck, gradually moving down her body. She did the same to him, and soon he found himself ready for more lovemaking. Time stood still, and the pleasure was all he thought about.

* * *

He woke as the birds started to sing and rose from the bed. Wren woke.

"I've got to go, Wren. I shouldn't have stayed so long, but we fell asleep. I only came to tell you what was happening."

She reached up and pulled him to her, kissing him, and once again stroking his back in the way he liked. "Can't you stay a bit longer? I've missed you so." Her mouth turned down and she wiped her eyes with the back of her hand.

Although he protested, Wren had her way. She knew exactly what to do to make it impossible for him to go. After more lovemaking, Carthinal managed to tear himself away.

The sun had risen and people were beginning to fill the streets as Carthinal approached Mabryl's house. The arch-mage would be up by now. Had his master missed him? What would he say? Would he refuse to teach him, now? After all, he had been insistent Carthinal stay in his house and had made a big thing about discipline.

As he approached the tree, he had climbed down, the door opened. Lillora emerged carrying a basket.

She stopped and put her hands on her hips. "Well, the truant returns."

Carthinal groaned. His escape had not gone undetected.

"Mabryl thought you'd decided not to learn. After all, it's hard work learning magic. You'd better go on in and see what he says."

Carthinal plodded up the steps and entered through the door Lillora had left open. He paused in the hallway, looking around.

Emmienne came rushing down the stairs. "Oh, you are in trouble! Mabryl is both anxious and angry at the same time." She grinned. "Where've you been? Going out at night to see a girl, were you? Who is she? Is she pretty?"

"Yes...no...er..."

"There you are!" Mabryl's voice came from the study. The man himself strode out, lips pressed together and hands clenched by his side. "What do you mean by sneaking out at night? What have I told you about magic needing discipline? It needs honesty, too. Where have you been that you needed to sneak out like that?"

Carthinal took a deep breath. He would be honest. His grandfather had taught him not to tell lies, and now Mabryl was talking about honesty. "I went to see my old mates. They needed to know where I am and what I'm doing. If they didn't know, they'd think I'd betrayed them and come after me."

"Hmm. You could have told me that. I understand." Mabryl's tone softened. "But no more of it. You have had no one to discipline you or teach you right from wrong for a long time. I expect no more of these night-time excursions." He swung round and entered his study. His voice came back. "Come and start today's lessons. More writing practice is needed."

Carthinal groaned and followed his master into the study. Writing and reading. Reading and writing. That's all he seemed to be doing. That and learning the names of plants and the stars. When was he going to learn some real magic?

CHAPTER SEVEN

THE DAYS PASSED. CARTHINAL READ THE BOOKS AND copied spells along with other things Mabryl gave him. Soon he was writing a fair hand, and his reading improved. Mabryl still made no move to teach him how to do any of the spells he copied.

His mind wandered as he read the books on the history of magic. What was the point of learning about things long past?

He voiced this to Mabryl one day.

"We need to remember what has gone before, and the results of these things," his mentor replied. "If not, we will be condemned to repeat the mistakes of those who went before us, and we can't enjoy the good things, either."

"Hmm. I suppose so." Carthinal went back to reading about how King Sauvern of Hambara united the warring kingdoms of Grosmer into one kingdom.

He still wanted to see his old friends, though. Especially Wren. They had been good to him and saved him from starvation. He could not forget them, and so, one night, several months after Mabryl had forbidden nightly excursions, he climbed out of his window once more.

He made his way to the Beasts' headquarters. Tapping on the door in the usual way, Porcupine let him in.

She grinned to see him, then frowned. "Wren thought you'd forgotten 'er. She's…"

"Never." Carthinal made his way along the hallway.

As he entered the main room, he spotted Wren on the other side. He called out to her.

She stopped what she was doing and stood stock still, eyes wide. Her hand flew to her mouth. "F…Fox!"

Carthinal frowned. Why did she look like that? Her attitude was not one of pleasure—more like fear. He'd never done anything to make her afraid, so what was going on?

"Hi, Wren. I managed to get out again. I had to be careful, though. Mabryl caught me last time, so I waited until he thought I was going to be a good boy."

Wren smiled, but Carthinal thought it looked a bit watery. This sentence in italics but not in bold.*Something's wrong.*

Cat entered and called to Wren. "Are you coming to bed?"

Carthinal whirled around. So that was the way it was. Cat had taken advantage of his long absence to steal his girl. Well, that was going to end right now.

As soon as Cat saw who stood there, he paused. Carthinal took the opportunity and reached his erstwhile friend in a second. He swung his fist and it met the other's chin. The small man staggered back but did not fall. He ducked in time to avoid Carthinal's next swing and rolled onto his legs, grabbing and pulling as he did so.

Carthinal fell heavily and Cat jumped on top of him.

The pair rolled around the large room, grappling each other and punching whenever the chance arose. Carthinal did not know how many of his punches hit, but he knew he sometimes hit the floor as his adversary rolled out of the way. Cat was agile while Carthinal had become a little unfit in the weeks spent with Mabryl.

A loud voice sounded. "What d'you think you're doin'? One of the rules 'ere is NO FIGHTIN'. At least, not where I can see."

It was Rooster. Hands grabbed both young men and pulled them apart. When Carthinal looked round, he found himself held by Bull, and Ox, another one of the Beasts' security men, detained Cat.

Rooster stood in front of them, hands on hips, looking at the pair through narrowed eyes.

Carthinal panted as he stood, unable to move out of Bull's grasp. He frowned and glared at Cat. He wanted to smash the small man's nose. How dare he take his girl?

Rooster was speaking, a severe look on his face. "Now, what's this about? Fox? Cat?"

Carthinal balled his fists again and pressed his lips together. He took a deep breath. "Cat took advantage of my long absence to take my girl."

Cat's eyes flashed. "You were gone for bleedin' months. We thought you'd decided life in th' comfort of a proper 'ouse were better'n wi' us, and 'ad gone over t' 'them'."

Carthinal struggled against Bull's iron grip.

"Wait," Rooster said. "Fox, did you say Cat had stolen your girl?"

Carthinal nodded. "Yes. Wren was my girl before he took her."

"Hmm!" Rooster looked at Cat. "What do you have to say?"

"What I just said. I thought—we all thought—Fox 'ad left us. I decided 'e didn't want Wren anymore. P'rhaps 'e'd found

54

someone else. 'E's got a pretty enough face for any woman ter want 'im."

Rooster sighed. "Didn't either of you think to ask Wren? She's not a piece of jewellery to be argued over. She 'as a mind and she uses it. She'll decide for 'erself 'oo she wants to be with. You can't make that decision for 'er, 'ooever wins the fight." He turned to Wren. "D'you want to be wi' either o' these two?"

Wren looked down at her feet, then at Cat. Carthinal felt his heart sink into his boots.

"Sorry, Cat. I'll take Fox. I thought 'e'd gone for good, you see. It's been so long."

She walked over to where Carthinal stood, still held by Bull. "Sorry, Fox." She leaned her head against him.

"Let 'em, go," Rooster said, and walked away.

Carthinal put his arm around Wren and held her tight. "I'm glad you chose me," he whispered.

Cat approached, glancing around. He stopped a good arm's length away from Carthinal.

He took a deep breath. "Please accept my apology, Wren. I shouldn't 'ave treated you like a possession."

"No, you shouldn't." She turned to Carthinal. "And neither should you."

Cat turned and walked away. After a few paces, he stopped and looked back. "Fox, we was good friends once. I 'ope we can be again, sometime."

Carthinal watched him go with a sad expression. He put an arm around Wren. "He's right. We were good friends. I shouldn't have hit him."

As usual, Carthinal's anger dissipated quickly and he went over to Rooster. "I apologise for causing a disruption. You're right. Wren is her own woman." He looked to the door where Cat had vanished, then turned back.

"This magic business is going to take longer than I thought. I've hardly even started. Mabryl won't let me start learning spells until I've learned discipline, he says."

Rooster looked him up and down, then tilted his head. "'E's right. It'd be dangerous to 'ave someone wi' an uncontrolled temper able to do magic. Think what you could 'ave done to Cat, and maybe others in the vicinity, if you 'ad spells at your fingertips. Go back to your Mabryl and stay there until you've learnt some control."

Carthinal hung his head. He looked at Wren, still at his side, and hugged her.

She looked up into his indigo eyes and sighed. "I think that was an order, Fox. I don't suppose I'll see you for quite some time, then."

"I can still come out at night and meet you."

She shook her head, looking sad. "No. That would be poor discipline. Rooster, and Mabryl, have both ordered you to learn. I promise I'll wait for you." She reached up and kissed him before turning away, tears in her eyes.

CHAPTER EIGHT

Carthinal came out of the study in Mabryl's house. He heard voices coming from the living room.

"I think you're mad, Mabryl. He's a wild kid from the streets."

"He's learning, Danu. He's stayed in at night for the last two months."

Carthinal realised that Mabryl was talking to Duke Danu, the ruler of the Duchy of Bluehaven. The duke had once been learning to be a mage, but his elder brother met with a fatal hunting accident. This meant Danu had to leave his studies as he was now the heir to the dukedom.

He had met Mabryl when they were both apprentices and kept an interest in magic. The two men were close friends.

"I thought it was a madcap idea when you took him on as an apprentice, but to consider adopting him..."

Carthinal knew he should not be listening to a private conversation, but he could not resist. It concerned him. And what was Mabryl saying about adopting him? Carthinal crept quietly to the door to hear more.

"—potential. I felt it when I saw him teach himself to do a simple cantrip. He could be a great mage one day."

"Maybe, but do you have to adopt him? He could get you into a lot of trouble."

"Danu, I have no wife, no children. What's going to happen to this when I leave this world?" He swept his hand around, indicating the large room and all it contained. "I don't want just anyone coming in and going through my magic stuff. It could be dangerous."

Carthinal crept away to his room. He needed to think. Italics, please, but not bold.*Do I want to be adopted? I've lived quite well up to now on my own.*

After he heard Danu leave, Mabryl called up the stairs. "Carthinal, come down here, please. Don't worry, you're not in trouble—for once."

Carthinal entered the living room and Mabryl told him to sit down.

"I've been talking to Duke Danu. I put an idea I had in front of him. I don't think he thought it a good one, but I still do, in spite of his arguments against it."

Carthinal shifted in his seat and kept his eyes downcast.

Mabryl told Carthinal about his plans to adopt him. "If I die without an heir, then all my things will revert to the Crown." He ran his hands through his hair. "You are an orphan, Carthinal. You have no one and nothing, so I thought of adopting you. This would be a help to us both. What do you think?"

Carthinal looked up. "Please may I think about this? It's a big step." His thoughts were in turmoil. What exactly would his adoption entail?

Mabryl nodded. "Of course. I wouldn't expect you to decide right away, but you do need to be fully in agreement. Now, you can go and think. I need to see some people who want their boy to become my apprentice, and I need to see what kind of potential he has."

Carthinal returned to his room. Mabryl's words span in his head.

Italics but not boldHe wants to adopt me. That means he'll be my father. Do I want to replace my real father? But then, he's been dead for years. I can only just remember him. And what about the gang? If I become his son, then I can hardly go around with a criminal gang, can I.

Then he remembered other words Mabryl had said.

Italics but not boldMabryl said I'd inherit everything he has. This house and all that's in it. That's worth a lot. Could we move the gang's HQ to here? No, that'd be no good. Can't have the Beasts in this district.

Mabryl told Duke Danu I have great potential. He said I could be a great mage. Did he mean that?

These thoughts and many others went round and round in his head until he thought he would go mad. It was a big decision. He dropped off to sleep to dream of an important quest where he used magic to fend off many dangers.

The next morning, before they ate breakfast, Carthinal cleared his throat.

"I did a lot of thinking last night after I went to bed. He swallowed and looked at his feet, then up at Mabryl. "I've decided that I would like you to adopt me."

Mabryl beamed. "It won't be straightforward, I don't suppose." He took the plate of eggs and bacon Lillora had brought in from the kitchen. "You are not a minor in the eyes of the law. I'm not quite sure exactly what your legal position is. You aren't an adult, though, no matter what the law states."

Carthinal took a plate and put an egg and some bacon onto it. He passed it to Emmienne who had entered the room. When she took it, he helped himself and pulled a chair up to the table. He took a bite of the bacon and reached for some toast.

Mabryl began to butter hisown toast and said, "Your age could be a problem. You appear to be only about fifteen, both physically and mentally, but in actual years, you are eighteen and an adult according to Grosmerian law. Elves attain their majority at twenty-five if I remember correctly. Humans at sixteen. As you have mixed parentage, I would guess that you would be the equivalent age at somewhere around twenty-one." Mabryl looked into the distance. "Perhaps we could tell the lawyer you are only fourteen."

Carthinal's eyebrows shot up. "A-are you saying we should lie to the lawyer?"

Mabryl looked away for a second before replying. "It's not really a lie. You are a half-elf and as a result, have developed slower than a human child. In human terms, you are about fifteen. We'll both need to go to the lawyer, so we can get all the details straight, including who your parents were."

Carthinal drew his brows together. "Which lawyer will you go to?"

"I've always used Gromblo Grimnor. He has a big practice in Bluehaven. He does very well if his apparent money is anything to go by."

*Italics but not bold**Can I persuade him to use a different lawyer? Or maybe I can give a different name for my parents. But if Gromblo recognises me, I'm in a lot of shit. And he'll expose Mabryl as a liar. He knows exactly how old I am.*

"When will we go to see him?" Carthinal asked.

"I need to find out exactly what we need to do first. I'll need to go to see him and ask him about the procedures before you come, too."

Carthinal nodded. He would have to think this one through. Gromblo would no doubt bring out the paper saying

Carthinal was dead, and then what? Mabryl would not believe a reprobate young man against a well-known lawyer. Especially one who had papers to prove it. He would have to somehow make sure those papers disappeared. But what about his name? Carthinal wasn't a common name in Grosmer, the country in which he lived. Much thought would be needed.

But not now.

They had all finished their breakfast and Mabryl wanted both his apprentices in his study. Today he was going to teach Carthinal a simple spell. Not a teaching spell, but one that would take more energy to manipulate the mana than he had used up until now.

Putting all thoughts of Gromblo to one side, Carthinal almost ran into Mabryl's study. This would be a momentous day. A real spell, not a little trick.

As he entered, Mabryl handed him a large book. It had a black cover with a red dragon engraved on the outside. The leather cover felt soft to his touch. Carthinal opened it and saw blank pages. He looked at Mabryl with raised eyebrows.

"It's your spellbook. You will write your spells in here as you find them. I suggest you divide it up into sections. Each section for one level of difficulty, so you don't get them mixed up, and you can easily find what you want."

Carthinal grinned as he caressed the spine of the book. "Thank you, Mabryl. This is a wonderful present. I promise I'll keep it tidy."

Emmienne bounced over. "That's so-o beautiful, Carthinal."

"You'll get one as soon as I think you're able to perform a real spell, not a learning trick. I don't know what to have on the front of a book for you, though. The dragon seemed right for Carthinal, somehow." He turned to Carthinal. "You must write the spell into your book before you even think about casting it."

Carthinal spent the next few hours painstakingly copying the magic words and the diagrams of the hand gestures needed to perform it.

Mabryl had given him the choice of spells to try. The young man had been thinking about the meeting with Gromblo and had decided on a course of action. He needed to decide which spell to choose to facilitate his plan.

He looked at the easy spells in Mabryl's spellbook, chose one and began the laborious task of copying. Everything had to be exactly right or the spell would not work. It took the rest of the morning.

When he had finished copying, Lillora called them in for lunch so Carthinal could not try out the spell for a while. He sat at the table fidgeting until Mabryl told him to stop. He forced himself not to bolt his food. Finishing before everyone would not make his spell attempt come more quickly.

CHAPTER NINE

After everyone finished eating, Mabryl took Carthinal into the back garden where he had a special building for practising spells. One where it did not matter if the spells damaged something.

"I'm rather surprised you chose this spell. Still, let's see how you get on with it."

With the book on a table in front of him, Carthinal carefully enunciated the words and moved his hands in the way he had drawn. Nothing happened.

"It's your pronunciation of 'brillogin'," Mabryl said. "You are putting the emphasis on the first syllable, and it should be on the middle one. Try again."

"Cambli suarim brillogin su."

As he said the words, Carthinal moved his fingers in a complex pattern.

This time, a fly that had been buzzing around the room dropped to the table.

"Hey! I did it!"

Mabryl laughed. "Yes. You managed to put a small fly to

sleep. But look at the mice in the cage. They're still wide-awake. Try again."

The fly was struggling to its feet as Carthinal chanted again. As it took off, it fell back onto the table, but this time, a spider dropped from the ceiling to join it.

Carthinal grinned. "Two this time."

"One last try. This time try to get at least one of the mice to go to sleep."

Carthinal tried again. This time one of the mice yawned and lay down as though exhausted but stayed awake.

The young man pursed his lips. "He didn't actually go to sleep."

"No, but he became very tired. Well done. That's good for a first attempt."

Carthinal leaned on the table. "I feel as if I've cast the spell on myself." He yawned.

"That's what magic does. It takes some of your energy. You will feel less tired as you gain more experience. This is why novices have to learn to perform the cantrips first—to build up their energy levels. This, in turn, allows them to hold more of the mana."

Carthinal kept on practising the spell. He managed to get one mouse to sleep and all the flies and spiders in the practice room.

A few days later, Mabryl came into the study where Carthinal and Emmienne worked on the tasks he had set them. Carthinal studied the moon phases—not an easy task with two moons orbiting the planet of Vimar at differing rates. Emmienne read a book about the history of Grosmer.

Mabryl removed his cloak and hung it on the pegs behind the door. "I've been to the lawyer, Carthinal. We can start the adoption procedure right away."

Looking up, Carthinal put his book on the table. "What will it entail?"

"Not much. The lawyer will need to know your name and that of your parents. There should be some evidence they are deceased, though. Do you know if there are any papers anywhere?"

Carthinal rubbed his hand over the beard, which was trying to grow. "I suppose my grandfather would have had the papers, but how we can find them...?" He shrugged.

*Italics, but not bold*I suspect Gromblo will have them. *They would have been in my grandfather's house when he stole it from me. No chance of getting them now.*

Carthinal pondered. A tricky situation. Since Gromblo had falsified his death certificate, he would not likely admit to him being the grandson of Kendo Borlin. He would bring out the death certificate and "prove" Carthinal was dead. What would Mabryl do then? Would he throw him out and refuse to teach him anymore?

As he probed himself, he realised he wanted to learn magic more than anything else. He enjoyed the feeling it gave him. Oh, yes, there was the power, but also a physical sensation. He wanted that again and again.

The next day he had decided what to do. The lessons dragged and when Mabryl dismissed his apprentices, Carthinal made his way out to the spell room.

He sat on a stool and did deep breathing exercises to prepare and drew as much of the mana as he could into himself. Closing his eyes, he concentrated on the sleep spell he planned to use.

He had caught a stray cat the previous day and put it in a cage. The cat was not pleased and clawed at the bars, trying to get out.

Carthinal opened his eyes and stared at the animal, then he began to chant. The mana built up inside him as he drew it in. He felt the mounting pressure demanding release, but he drew more. He now held more of the mana than he had ever done before. He held it as long as he could, then released it towards the cat.

The animal yawned and laid its head on the cage floor as it fell sound asleep. Simultaneously, all the spiders, flies and also a small sparrow fell from the rafters. When he looked in the cages, all the creatures Mabryl kept for the magical training of his pupils had fallen asleep.

He plopped onto the stool, panting. He had put every-thing to sleep. And he had held more mana than ever before. He put his head onto his arms, exhausted.

* * *

He decided to execute his plan that evening after they had eaten, hoping he had managed to recover sufficiently. That should give him enough time. With any luck, he would not need any magic.

In the evenings, Mabryl allowed his apprentices time to themselves. Carthinal stood and thanked Lillora for an excel-lent meal, then left the room. His stomach churned at the thought of what he planned to do. He had done worse with the gang, though. Why was he so anxious this time? There was no danger.

He set off toward the city centre to where Gromblo had his office. The streets did not have the bustle of people that milled around during the day. Most folk were now eating, or had just finished and were settling down to an evening at home.

Approaching the office, he was shocked to see the flick-ering of a light in the window. He had to get into that office to destroy the false document, so he crept up to the window and peered in. Sure enough, there was Gromblo sitting at his desk, rustling papers in front of him.

As Carthinal watched, the man rose and went to a cabinet where he fumbled around before putting the papers inside. His heart was beating so hard he thought Gromblo would surely hear it. Indeed, the man did look toward the window before leaving the office.

Hearing the outer door of the building close, Carthinal stood and tried the window. Locked! He took a thin piece of metal from his pocket and pushed it up between the frame. It was a sash window, and he hoped to get the piece of metal to push the catch open. He would then be able to lift the bottom pane and gain access.

Tongue protruding, the young man wiggled the metal from side to side until it reached the latch.

Again, more wiggling, pushing and pulling, until he heard laughter and footsteps coming toward him. Pulling the metal from the window, Carthinal slipped back into the shadows. He watched as a young couple strolled up the street.

They paused opposite where Carthinal stood holding his breath and kissed. He watched as the young man's hand strayed to the girl's breast. Surely they weren't going to make love here? That would mess his plans up good and proper.

The girl giggled. "Not here, someone might come. Let's go to the park."

Carthinal let out his breath as they hurried away, anxious for their lovemaking. He crossed to the window once again.

This time the metal made contact with the latch. He pushed it to one side, which proved to be more difficult than he had anticipated. Then he felt movement.

Replacing the metal in his pocket, he lifted the window and slipped in to find the false document.

Standing in the centre of the room, Carthinal turned around. How could he locate this one document? Gromblo must have a system for filing. Was it alphabetical, or some other system known only to Gromblo and his secretary? He would only find out by looking.

He opened a drawer stuffed full of papers. The first one he took out belonged to someone called Holind Morrin. He looked farther into the files. Here was one belonging to Brinswopple Ordin.

He shuffled the papers, and sure enough, there were names beginning with N between the two he had already found.

He does have them in alphabetical order. And by surname. Now I just have to find B.

He searched the various cupboards. It did not take him long to find the name, Borlin. He riffled through the file and found his death certificate. As he pulled the false document from the drawer, he heard the unlocking of a door.

He frowned and slipped behind one of the cupboards, document in hand.

The door opened and Gromblo walked in, muttering to himself. "Stupid me to leave things behind. How could I forget?"

He stopped in his tracks as a draught from the window struck him.

"I didn't leave that open! I looked before I left. Someone must have been in here." He strode to the window and closed it.

Carthinal watched as the lawyer opened drawer after drawer, checking its contents. When he came to the one containing Holind Morrin, he paused and looked around the room, frowning. He began to put the papers back in order, muttering.

He pulled some out, looked at them and walked to the window. Once nearer the light, he held the papers towards it. Then sighing in irritation, he returned to his desk.

Lifting a candle, he took out a flint, struck a spark and lit it. He read the paper in the light from the candle and nodded. Still holding the candle and the paper, Gromblo approached the cupboard behind which Carthinal crouched.

Carthinal muttered the words of magic. This was why he had learned the spell and practised it so hard—in case he were disturbed in his venture. Would he be able to put a grown man to sleep, though? He would only use it as a last resort.

As he walked toward the cupboard, Gromblo tripped and grabbed its edge for balance. This made it move enough for him to see Carthinal's foot. He lunged as Carthinal released his spell. Almost immediately, the lawyer yawned and sank to the floor in a deep sleep, dropping the papers he held.

Carthinal knew his spell would not last long. Being a novice at casting spells, he was lucky to have managed to get Gromblo to sleep at all. Now he must hurry and destroy the false document he had found.

Tired though he felt after casting the spell, Carthinal ran to the window, paper in hand. He wrestled it open, leapt through and closed it behind him. Once outside, he muttered the words for the spell to give a small flame and set fire to the false death certificate. It burned to ash and the blackened bits of paper blew away in the wind.

CHAPTER TEN

THE NEXT MORNING, MABRYL ANNOUNCED HE HAD AN appointment with Gromblo and that Carthinal was to go with him this time, to sort out the details.

Carthinal shivered. Gromblo had seen him last night. Would he recognise him as the thief who had broken in? Would he recognise him as Carthinal, grandson of Kendo Borlin?

He considered feigning illness, but he would have to face this sometime. The worst that could happen was that Mabryl might refuse to teach him. He could always return to the Beasts. Perhaps he could steal a simple spellbook from Mabryl and learn on his own.

Carthinal took his time getting ready to leave.

"Come on, Carthinal. We'll be late," Mabryl called. "Gromblo hates people who are late. If we want a favourable outcome, we must be on time."

Carthinal came down the stairs, dragging his feet.

Mabryl put his head on one side. "Are you having second thoughts? I don't want to go through with this adoption unless you are completely in favour."

"No, Mabryl. I'm sorry. Let's go."

Italics but not bold.The sooner we see Gromblo, the better, then I'll know what my future holds.

Calling to Lillora that they were about to leave, Mabryl opened the front door and the pair turned their feet toward the centre of the town.

Halfway there, Mabryl sniffed. "Smells like smoke. Someone must have been burning rubbish."

When they arrived in the street where Gromblo had his office, the source of the smell became clear. Gromblo's office was a smouldering shell.

"Goodness. What's happened here?" Mabryl exclaimed.

Men with buckets threw water onto the building and those next to it to prevent any sparks from setting light to the surrounding buildings. Fire was a very real danger in Bluehaven, and in most towns, as the buildings were constructed of wooden frames interspersed with brick.

If the wood burned, then the brick structure would collapse. With buildings containing so much wood, it was easy for a spark to ignite adjacent buildings. A butcher's shop, next to Gromblo's office, had a few scorched places, but the bucketwielding men had managed to save it. Not so Gromblo's office.

A heap of rubble lay where the building had once stood with little wisps of smoke still rising from some of the wood.

Carthinal paled. He had not intended this. It must have been the candle Gromblo was carrying. He had not thought about that when he put Gromblo to sleep. All he had thought about was escape and destroying the false death certificate. He looked around, his eyes casting this way and that to see if there was any chance anyone could have seen and recognised him last night. Gromblo would when he arrived. The young man slipped behind his mentor.

Mabryl spotted someone he knew and hailed the man.

"What happened here? I had an appointment this morning with Gromblo." He glanced around. "Where is he, anyway? He should be here. After all, his office has burned down."

The other man shook his head. "You must have only just arrived. They found Gromblo's body in the building."

Carthinal's hand flew to his mouth. All he had wanted to do was to burn the false death certificate so Mabryl did not think he was an impostor. He had not intended to kill Gromblo.

Mabryl continued talking. "What was he doing there at that time of night?"

The other man shrugged. "Who knows? But I overheard someone saying his wife told the guard he had returned to find some papers he needed today. He wanted to look over them."

Italics but not boldWere they the papers referring to me? Had Mabryl told him my name and he wanted to check he had the death certificate? Why had he not told Mabryl of my death? Or was it something else entirely?

A small group gathered around Mabryl and his friend. Carthinal slipped back, trying not to be noticed.

"They think he lit a candle and fell asleep while reading," a woman said. "The guard found the remains of a candle near his body. There's something funny about it though. He wasn't sitting at his desk when they found him, so how did he fall asleep?"

Another woman said, "I always thought there was something shady about that man and never trusted him. I wouldn't be surprised if it wasn't someone who he'd cheated in some way, having his revenge."

A tall man said, "He was a clever lawyer, though. He got my brother off a theft charge when it looked as if he would be found guilty." He looked around the gathered group. "He was innocent, of course, but it was thanks to Gromblo he didn't go to jail."

A girl of around sixteen spoke up. "I walked past the back of here last night when it had gone dark. The office was still standing then."

A guard heard this and came over. "Did you say you were here last night?"

"Only passing, sir."

"Did you see anyone hanging around?"

A young man around the same age spoke up. "I did."

Carthinal went cold at hearing this. Shivers ran up and down his spine. He closed his eyes and took a deep breath.

"Who was it? Would you recognise them again?" The guard turned his attention to the young man.

"He was about..." He looked around, and his eyes fell on Carthinal. "About as tall as that chap there."

"Anything else?"

"I thought it a bit odd—him hanging about in the shadows, but took no more notice. I was with my girl, see?"

"We went to the park," the girl replied, "and didn't see any more."

There were sniggers from some of the crowd.

"Well, that's not much help. Could've been almost anyone. Anyway, the likelihood is that it was a tragic accident."

Carthinal closed his eyes and sent up a quick prayer to Majora, the goddess of magic. If the authorities thought it was an accident, then he would not be suspected. But what had the woman said about Gromblo's body not being at his desk? Would that make them think it wasn't an accident?

Carthinal's heart was beating so hard he thought it might jump out of his chest. He felt sick, and tears pricked at the back of his eyes.

*Italics but not bold*Why did I think burning the document was a good idea? Oh, if only I could go back in time. I'd do things differently. I'd make sure the candle was out before I left. I would have had time.

He felt weak, and his legs shook as he sidled up to Mabryl. "What happens now?"

Mabryl turned worried eyes to him. "This is a terrible tragedy, Carthinal. Gromblo was the best lawyer in Blue-haven. The poor man. I hope he didn't suffer. Sometimes people die from the smoke, not from being burned. Let's hope this was the case with Gromblo, and that he was dead before the flames reached him."

Carthinal nodded. He could not find his voice to speak. He had killed a man. Not in a fair fight, but by carelessness and stupidity. What he had done in the gang fights didn't count—it wasn't the same. It was fight or be killed himself. Anyway, he couldn't be sure he'd actually killed anyone then. This time was different. He was entirely culpable.

He heard a voice from the past in his head. A voice from a dream. 'When you meet problems, always think them through. Take your time, and don't try to rush things. If you do that, things will usually turn out right in the end.'

He had not done that. He had not thought things through, and it had resulted in disaster.

"Can we go home?" he said in a small voice.

Mabryl looked at his pale face. "This has shocked you more than I would have thought. Death is always sad, but this seems to have affected you badly." He placed his hand on Carthinal's arm. "It's the thought of him dying in such horrible circumstances, I expect. Yes, we should go home. We need to find another lawyer, but sadly, none are as good as Gromblo."

CHAPTER ELEVEN

LATER THAT DAY, CARTHINAL SAT IN MABRYL'S STUDY, head in his hands. Mabryl had gone out, and he was supposed to be working, but he could not keep his mind on it.

"What's wrong, Carthinal?" Emmienne asked. "You've seemed out of sorts ever since you and Mabryl got back earlier. Not coming down with something are you?"

"What? Oh, no. I don't think so. I'm just...well, thinking."

She returned to her task, and Carthinal went back to brooding. Every now and then, he felt her eyes on him.

Italics but not boldWhat if that couple decides they could remember what I look like? No. They were too interested in each other. Did I drop anything that might point to the fact I was there? No, I don't think so.

He picked up the book again and tried to read, but the words swam in front of his eyes. If only he had not gone to retrieve that document. He could have found the guard who had helped Gromblo throw him out all those years ago. The guard knew the document was false. But would he help Carthinal? He had been accepting bribes, after all.

All these thoughts went round and round in his head. Part

of him was not sorry that Gromblo was dead. The man was a crook, lawyer or not. He was the reason Carthinal ended up on the streets. For all the lawyer cared, Carthinal could have died.

The young man sighed and closed his eyes. No, he was not sorry the man was dead. He had gone to Kalhera, goddess of death to be judged.

He rubbed his eyes, then, ignoring the book, leant back in his chair and closed them.

Mabryl walked in. He hung his coat on the stand in the corner.

"Still brooding?" he said, looking at Carthinal. "You look as if you'd killed him yourself. And don't worry, it won't stop the adoption. There are other lawyers who can sort it out."

Just then the knocker on the door banged. A few minutes later, Lillora knocked on the study door. Mabryl went to open it.

"It's a guard," she said. "He wants to talk to you and Carthinal."

Carthinal went cold and the colour drained from his face. Had they found something linking him to the fire?

Mabryl beckoned. "Come on, Carthinal. We'd better go and talk to the man. Not that we can help in any way."

Carthinal slowly rose and followed Mabryl through to the hall, pictures of the hangman in his head.

"What can we do for you?" Mabryl asked.

"You had an appointment with Gromblo this morning?"

Mabryl nodded. "Yes, but the office was a shell by the time we got there."

"Can you tell me what your appointment was about? I understand you had your apprentice with you."

"Yes. I plan to adopt him. He's an orphan, you see, and I have no family, so I thought it would be good for us both."

"I see," the guard said. "Did you notice anything when you got to the office?"

"Like what?" Mabryl asked.

Carthinal shuffled his feet and looked at the ground, the door, the ceiling, anywhere to avoid the guard's eyes. He waited for the accusation.

"I don't know. Anything that struck you as odd." He turned to Carthinal. "Did you notice anything?"

Carthinal shook his head. His tongue cleaved to the roof of his mouth and he could not speak.

"Come on, Carthinal," Mabryl said. "It's not like you to be lost for words."

The guard laughed. "Being questioned sometimes affects people like that. An otherwise loquacious person will become tongue-tied. If someone has a guilty conscience, it often has that effect."

Carthinal looked up sharply. What did this guard know? Had someone else been there?. Someone he had not seen, but who knew him?

The guard continued speaking. "We're simply asking around. We think it was an accident, but we need to make sure." He scratched his head. "The person the young couple saw must have made off. Perhaps he was planning on burglary but saw Gromblo returning so gave up the idea. That's the most likely, I think. But Gromblo might have had some enemies. Who knows? Are you sure you noticed nothing in the ruins, young man?"

Carthinal had found his voice again. "No, sir. Only the smell of burning. And everything being wet from the firemen."

"Well, I'll not trouble you any further, Archmage. We're questioning everyone who was at the scene, in case someone noticed something we've missed. But as I said, a terrible accident. Let's hope it teaches everyone in the city to take care with candles."

He saluted, and Mabryl let him out of the door.

Carthinal let out his breath. So they were thinking along the lines of an accident. If that was the case, he was in the clear. But he kept on seeing Gromblo's face and had the smell of burning in his nostrils for months afterwards.

CHAPTER TWELVE

Mabryl asked around, and friends told him of a new lawyer in town called Halor Prinkerson. He was supposed to be almost as good as Gromblo, they said. Mabryl contacted the new man to see if he would deal with his adoption of Carthinal.

Halor Prinkerson was only too pleased to take the job. He grinned at Mabryl. "It will be an honour, Archmage. Is this the young man you want to adopt?"

"Yes. His name is Carthinal. He is my apprentice." Mabryl smiled at the lawyer.

"What about relatives? Does he have any?"

Mabryl looked at Carthinal. His indigo eyes had darkened as he pressed his lips together. He must not allow his anger to escape that the questions had not been addressed to him.

Mabryl looked at Carthinal, nodding to him to reply.

"No. None that I know of," Carthinal said. I don't know my grandparents in Rindissillaron, so they don't count.

"Do you have any papers?" Halor now spoke directly to Carthinal, getting the message that the young man wanted to speak for himself.

Carthinal shook his head.

"Hmm! That makes it more difficult." The lawyer frowned and tapped his fingers on the desk. "How is it you have no papers? Everyone is supposed to have papers."

Mabryl took over. "He is an orphan. Until I took him as an apprentice, he lived on the streets. "

"Why did you decide to take him in, Archmage? Few people take these kids off the streets. They're wild and untameable." The lawyer looked perplexed.

Mabryl sighed and rolled his eyes. Even his patience was becoming strained. He glanced at Carthinal, knowing how easy it was to raise the young man's temper. Carthinal was sitting looking at his shoes.

"He has great potential for magic. I spotted that and wanted to train him. People who have such potential and are not trained are a danger to themselves and the people around them."

"I see." Halor jotted something down on a piece of paper. He turned to Carthinal again. "Do you remember anything of your parents?"

Carthinal blinked away the water that filled his eyes, then drew in a deep breath. "I can just remember them. My father went to fight in the Elven War of Succession. He never came back. My mother died of a broken heart not long afterward."

Mabryl reassuringly patted Carthinal's arm, then turned to Halor. "With such a tragic past, he had more to think about than papers. Staying alive was his priority."

Halor pursed his lips. "There's a good chance he's wanted by the guard if he was a street kid. I don't know if I want to get involved, just in case."

Mabryl shook his head. "Wouldn't it be better if I could save him from himself? If I could manage to reform him? I don't believe he's so entrenched in criminal life that he can't be turned around." He smiled at Halor. "Besides, I can make it worth your while."

Carthinal turned his head to where Mabryl sat, his eyes wide in amazement. Did he hear correctly? Was Mabryl offering a bribe? And to a lawyer, at that.

His eyes turned to his mentor, then to the lawyer who gave a brief nod and smiled. He drew some paper over and began to write.

He looked up. "Hmm. Carthinal is an unusual name."

The young man held his breath. Does Halor Prinkerson know Carthinal was the name of Kendo Borlin's grandson? If he does, then he will likely know of my supposed death. If he puts two and two together, he will no doubt think I'm trying to pull a fast one on Mabryl to get at his money.

Prinkerson began to write, then he looked up. "I've not been in Bluehaven for long," he said, "and I'm still learning about the people here. No doubt my predecessor would know all about you, Archmage, but please, will you give me some details?"

Carthinal suppressed a smile at hearing this. He was safe.

"I am, as you see, an archmage. I do quite a lot of work for the Duke when he wants something magical done. I also search out youngsters with the potential for magic, to train them. I have two apprentices at the moment—Carthinal, here, and a girl called Emmienne. Both have great potential."

Halor nodded and wrote something on the paper. When he had finished writing, he pushed the paper across the table towards Mabryl. "You need to sign here to say you've agreed to adopt Carthinal."

As Mabryl took the paper and began to read, Halor turned to the young man, who was fidgeting in his chair.

"You will need to sign to say you've agreed to be adopted." The lawyer ran his fingers through his hair and frowned. "Usually it would be whoever has been acting as your guardian, but in this case, Mabryl has been looking after you and he's adopting you." He smiled. "He can't very well sign both parts. You can make your mark when Mabryl has finished reading it and has signed it."

Mabryl looked up from reading the document. "Carthinal is my apprentice. Apprentice mages need to be able to read and write. Carthinal will sign it with his name after he has read it."

Prinkerson nodded then made a copy of the document, and all parties signed this second copy. Calling his secretary, Prinkerson had her file it and then stood. He handed the original document to Mabryl. "Congratulations, Archmage. You now have a son. It was a pleasure doing business with you. I hope we can offer you help in the future."

He turned to Carthinal. "And you have a father and a name. Congratulations, Carthinal Mabrylson."

* * *

The pair made their way back to Mabryl's home.

Once there, Mabryl took the certificate of adoption and rolled it carefully. He inserted it into a scroll case and placed it on a shelf in his study.

"I'm putting this here, Carthinal. If you ever need it, that's where you'll find it."

Carthinal's conscience pricked him over Gromblo's death but he pushed those thoughts down. Gromblo had been a dishonest man. Thanks to him, Carthinal had lost everything. He could have died, but now Mabryl had given him a new chance at life. He resolved from that moment that he would endeavour to live as his new father would expect. He owed him everything.

Lillora had made a special meal to celebrate, and as they sat around the table, Carthinal felt more at home than he had since his grandfather's death. He now had a home and a family.

AFTERWORD

I hope you enjoyed reading this story of Carthinal's early life.

I would very much appreciate it if you would leave an honest review. If you liked it, I will be delighted, but if you did not, please be honest. I can take it!

Reviews are important to authors in order to get their books noticed amid the many millions. The more reviews an author gets, the more her books will be brought to readers' attention.

If you would like to find out more about Carthinal and what happens to him later, you can read The Wolves of Vimar series.

Book 1, The Wolf Pack, *can be bought by following this link.*
http://mybook.to/TheWolfPack
Book 2, The Never-Dying Man
http://mybook.to/TheNeverDyingMan
Book 3, Wolf Moon
http://mybook.to/WolfMoonVM
The first prequel. Jovinda and Noli The story of Carthinal's parents.
http://mybook.to/jovinda

CONNECT WITH THE AUTHOR

You can connect with me on the following platforms.
My website and blog. http://aspholessaria.wordpress.com
My page at Next Chapter Publishing:
https://www.nextchapter.pub/authors/vm-sang
Facebook.
https://www.facebook.com/profile.php?
id=100008382226632
Goodreads.
https://www.goodreads.com/author/show/7246316.V_M_Sang
My Amazon Author Page.
https://www.amazon.co.uk/-/e/B00CK8JHRM
Instagram.
https://www.instagram.com/v.m.sang/

ACKNOWLEDGMENTS

I would like to thank everyone at Next Chapter who have worked so hard to bring this tale to you, especially Miika Hannila and the editors. They have done a stirling job.

Also, the book designers, who produce amazing covers for all Next Chapter publications.

A BIT ABOUT ME

I was born in Northwich in Cheshire, UK. and grew up in an idyllic area for children. My friends and I used to go out to play in the woodlands around the area.

While I was growing up, I was a tomboy. I climbed trees, played hide and seek in the woods, dammed the streams, searched for caterpillars and butterflies, learned about the birds and wild animals and picked wildflowers. (That was not illegal then, of course.)

When I grew up, I went to teacher training college where I studied Science with Maths and English as subsidiary subjects.

I took up painting and a variety of crafts during the time when I was bringing up my children. I still do them when not writing. One of my favourites is tatting, a craft that not many people seem to do these days, which is a pity as it's quite easy and makes many very pretty things.

I now live in East Sussex with my husband and enjoy the company of my grandchildren

.